THICKER THAN WATER

ANNE CASSIDY

To my mum, Alice Cassidy, who loves this
uch as I do

First published in 2016 in Great Britain by
Barrington Stoke Ltd
18 Walker Street, Edinburgh, EH3 7LP

www.barringtonstoke.co.uk

A CIP catalogue record for this book is available from the British Library upon request

ISBN: 978-1-78112-511-3

Printed in China by Leo

CONTENTS

1

LAST DAY IN BRIGHTON

George didn't know it was going to be his last day in Brighton.

He was standing next to Lennie on the seafront while Lennie stared at George's phone. Lennie's red baseball cap cast a shadow over his face as he prodded and jabbed at the screen. He made noises, little grunts and sighs – *Oh! Ah! Got it!*

They weren't due back at work until five, which meant that Lennie had two hours to go on the rides at the fun fair. His favourite was the Waltzer. He'd spend all day on it if he could, twisting and turning at breakneck speed. George had to keep an eye on him in case he got too excited. Lennie was 22 years old and nearly two metres tall, but he acted like a big kid.

"Give me my phone back now," George said. "Keep out of trouble. Don't stare at anyone."

"I won't," Lennie said.

As Lennie walked away, George kept his eye on the red baseball cap. There were hundreds of other people around, but George could see Lennie no matter where he went. That's why George liked the fun fair. He could relax. He bought a can of Fanta and sat down on a wall to check out a few sites selling rare vinyl on his phone.

A sudden loud shout made George turn his head to see where it had come from. The Dodgems. There was another squeal and George spotted Lennie. He was standing far too close to a girl with long blonde hair.

"He keeps touching my dress!" the girl shouted. Her face was blotchy and twisted with distress.

"I like the colour ..." Lennie said. "I just wanted to feel it."

The girl had on a silky red dress with a pattern of white birds. Lennie had grabbed the skirt and he was holding the bunched up fabric in his hand. As the girl backed away from him, the dress was pulled between them.

Lennie's eyes darted from the girl and back to George, but still he held onto the dress. George could see that the thin fabric was about to tear. He could see, too, the fear in Lennie's eyes. He put his hand over Lennie's and pulled at his fingers, but they were tight like a knot.

"Let it go, Lennie," George said. "Come on, mate. We need to get out of here."

George saw three guys run over from the other side of the fun fair. He knew who they were. They came in the pub where George and Lennie worked all the time and one of them had a nasty habit of punching people he didn't like.

At last George felt Lennie's fingers uncurl and let go of the girl's dress. George shoved him along and they ran out of the fair, raced along the seafront and turned off into a side street.

"Hurry up," George shouted.

But Lennie was too slow to keep up and he was well behind. George stopped and waited, all the time looking back down the road to see who was coming. Then he saw the other guys turn the corner. Their faces were red and angry and there were four of them now.

"This way," George said. He grabbed Lennie's arm and dragged him down an alley. There was a skip by a back gate, full of wood and bricks and old tiles.

George's breath was ragged and his heart was thumping. "Get in the skip," he panted.

Lennie moved some big bits of wood and climbed in. George pulled a sheet of wood over the top of him and made sure he was covered up. Then George scrambled in too and hid under an old kitchen cupboard.

From their hiding place inside the skip, George could hear footsteps and voices. He stretched his hand out and touched Lennie's arm so that Lennie knew to be quiet. When George was there Lennie did what he was told. George closed his mouth tight against the taste of cement dust.

The footsteps came closer and George heard voices clearly now.

I'll kill that moron!

He's a big bloke. More like he'd kill you.

There're four of us. We can break his legs.

We can give him a proper kicking.

Where are they?

They must have run back to the beach. We'll get them there.

And then George heard their footsteps moving away.

After a while Lennie whispered, "Have they gone?"

Yes, they had gone, but George didn't answer. The rubbish in the skip pressed down on him, the dust made him feel as if he couldn't breathe. How many times had Lennie got him into a mess like this?

They'd been in Brighton for six weeks without any trouble. He'd thought they might stay there.

Now they would have to move on and find somewhere new to live.

2
ON THE ROAD

George and Lennie got off the bus a mile outside Hastings. They had all their rucksacks and bags with them, and in one hand George was carrying his record case. The case was heavy, but he didn't trust Lennie with it. The records inside were worth a fortune.

They walked along the coast road. On one side there were houses and on the other neat green grass, flower beds and wooden benches. Beyond that was the sea. The water was choppy with white froth on the waves, blown about by a warm evening breeze. The low sun looked like an orange that you could pick out of the sky and eat.

George had got off the bus early for a reason. He wanted to talk to Lennie about Hastings. They couldn't afford to get into trouble again. It was August and he wanted them to stay in one place and get some money together before the winter. In George's pocket was a card that a guy from the hostel in Brighton had given him. It said –

The Old Ship Inn – Billy Bell.

The Old Ship was a pub in Hastings that was looking for someone to DJ on Saturday nights. Billy Bell was the landlord and he was a bit of a crook but he paid cash-in-hand, so George was prepared to put up with that.

"George, look," Lennie said. "A burger van. Can I have a hot dog?"

The burger van was in the middle of the grass. A sign on the top said, "Snack Attack".

"But I'll only have a hot dog if they have ketchup," Lennie said.

"They all have ketchup, Lennie."

But Lennie didn't listen. "If they don't have ketchup I won't have one."

"They will have ketchup. Go and get us one each. And a Sprite."

"I will," Lennie said. "And I'll get some ketchup for you, promise."

George sat on a bench next to a big old tree and watched as Lennie went up to the woman at the hatch. He must have asked her about ketchup because she picked up a big red bottle and showed it to him.

A couple of minutes later Lennie came back with the food. George was looking at a heart that had been carved into the bark of the tree. It seemed fresh, as if someone had done it in the last few days, and it made him think of his old girlfriend. Lauren. She'd have liked it if he'd carved hearts into tree trunks for her. But George would never have thought to do that – he was no good at that sort of stuff.

He ate his hot dog and drank his Sprite.

His record case was wedged between his feet, and its dark red leather shone in the sun. It was a nice one – it had been his dad's and so George got it when his dad died. He kept his dad's best records stacked up inside.

George knew that he was a good DJ – he'd worked the pubs in London a few nights a week, but in Brighton he'd only done a few sets. The rest of the time he'd spent clearing up glasses in the pub while Lennie did the heavy work.

Now they had to start again.

Lennie was staring out at the sea, munching on his hot dog and humming a tune in between bites. George put his hand on his arm to get his attention.

"Look at this place," he told him. "This bench and the tree and the burger van. Try and remember it. The van is called Snack Attack and, look, the tree has a heart carved on it."

"I like this place," Lennie said. "I like the burger van."

"The burger van might be closed sometimes, or gone," George told him. "But look at the tree. Look at the heart."

Lennie got up and used his fingers to trace out the heart.

"Why is a heart on the tree?" he asked.

"Somebody took their knife and carved it. For a girl."

"A heart," Lennie said. "It's nice."

"So, you'll remember this place," George said. "And if anything ever goes wrong then you come here and wait for me. Even if you're here for a long time you still wait for me."

"You'll come, George?"

"I'll come," George said. "I'll always come. You just sit here and wait."

"I'll wait, George."

George felt a lump in his throat and blinked back a sudden tear. Lennie would wait all day and all night if he asked him to. He'd do anything for him. George knew he should be pleased, but Lennie often felt like a heavy weight he needed to carry day in and day out.

3
THE OLD SHIP INN

Billy Bell was a big beefy man with a wide chest. He had on a waistcoat that didn't quite button up and his shirt sleeves were folded back. George could see the strong muscles in his arms as he pulled a pint from behind the bar in the Old Ship Inn. Even his dark hair was strong and thick, and wiry like a brush.

George handed over the card.

"Yeah, I had a call about you," Billy Bell said. "You can use the decks and you've got your own records?"

George nodded. "I have. Lots of different stuff. Gets everyone dancing."

"Not too much dancing," Billy said. "I want them buying drinks at the bar."

"Course."

Billy looked at Lennie. "And what do you do while he's playing records?"

George jumped in as fast as he could. "He's strong," he said. "He can carry crates of beer, change barrels. He's an all-round handyman. He can do anything."

"Why not let him speak for himself?" Billy turned to face Lennie. "How old are you?"

Lennie looked at George. George mouthed *twenty-two*.

"Twenty-two," Lennie said.

"You look younger," Billy said.

"No, he's twenty-two," George said. "He's my cousin so I know."

Billy looked back at George with a frown on his face, as if he suspected them of something bad.

"How old are you?" he asked George.

"I'm 19, nearly twenty. I've got a passport here if you want to see it."

Billy shook his head.

"We don't need paperwork here," he said. "This bar runs on trust. You work for me, I expect loyalty."

"Sure," George said. "Of course. It's cash in hand?"

"That's how I work. That suit you?"

"Yes."

"What about your cousin?"

George looked at Lennie. He was smiling at a smaller, younger man who was sorting out bottles of beer further along the bar. The man had noticed. He stopped what he was doing and glared at Lennie.

"Are you laughing at me?" he said.

"He's not," George said. "He's not even looking at you. He's thinking of something else."

"He's taking the mick!" the man said.

"Trust me, he's not," George said. "Lennie, mate, wait outside."

Lennie shrugged and walked off. The door banged shut behind him.

"He's not like other people," George said. "He doesn't always understand stuff. I look after him. We work together, travel together. We're family."

The younger man was still standing with his arms folded across his chest, but Billy nodded.

"OK," he said. "I approve of that. Family is important. As long as he doesn't cause any trouble he can stay. There's a room at the top of the pub you can have for a couple of weeks – see how it goes." He turned to the other man and nodded at him. "This is my son. We call him Boxer because he used to be a fighter. Won cups and that, when he was a kid."

Boxer scowled at George as if he was about to put his fists up.

"Thanks," George said, with a wary look at Boxer. "You won't regret it."

4
THE DREAM

George gave Lennie the bed nearest the window and then he unpacked their bags. It didn't take long – there wasn't much to sort. The only thing he didn't unpack was his record case.

Lennie opened the window and looked out. He was humming his usual tune. He had already forgotten the man in the bar.

"Look, George, dogs!" Lennie said and pointed out of the window.

The back yard of the pub was full of old barrels and crates, but in the corner was a big cage with two dogs in it. One was asleep and the other was gnawing at a bone it held between its paws.

George frowned. Lennie liked dogs, but he would get upset if anything happened to them.

"What do you think their names are?" Lennie said.

"I don't know," George said. "Shut the window." And then, to distract him, "You want to play that game on my phone?"

"Sure!"

In seconds Lennie's thumb was moving back and forth as he played his favourite game. It was made for kids, but he loved it.

George sighed. Sometimes Lennie was easy to look after. But sometimes he was a pain.

When George was 13, Lennie came to live with him and his dad. He went to the same school for a while and George had to keep an eye on him. Lennie was 16, but he wasn't streetwise – far from it. Other kids were always picking on him and taking his money off him. George often saw him down the far end of the playground getting battered and bruised by some older kid. The worst offender was a boy called Jordan Bishop, who would stride around the playground looking for Lennie so he could pick on him.

After a few months of this, George got fed up. He took Lennie and they went and found Jordan Bishop behind the drama studio. Jordan's mates were there and they started on Lennie straight away, taking his bag, chucking his books about, shoving him around. George tried to tell them that Lennie wasn't like other kids, that it wasn't a fair contest. George even said that if Jordan left Lennie alone he would give him money every week. Jordan Bishop just laughed in his face.

George had done everything he could to settle it with words. In the end he had no choice.

"Just hit him, Lennie," he said. "Hit him hard."

Lennie stepped forward and punched Jordan Bishop. He just kept going, like a machine. George had to step in.

"Stop! That's enough, Lennie. Stop now!"

Lennie stopped dead.

Jordan Bishop was curled up on the ground with his arms crossed round his middle and blood oozing from his mouth.

No one bothered Lennie after that.

Then, when he was 18, Lennie left school and went to work with George's dad on a building site. That lasted for two years until George's dad fell from some scaffolding high up against the side of an old house.

In the hospital George sat by his dad's bed. The fall had broken his dad's skull and smashed all his insides up. He wasn't going to get better.

George held his dad's hand and felt how light it was. The power was all gone from it, and the skin was like paper. The weaker it got the tighter George held it. Just before midnight was the last time he heard his dad's voice. *Take care of Lennie, George. Promise me you will.* He looked at his dad's face but his eyes were shut and his mouth was closed tight. Had he said it? George wasn't sure. His dad was dead and now the words were in George's head and no one could take them back.

Lennie cried for weeks. Months. Social services got involved and George was afraid they'd put him into foster care, so one night he and Lennie slipped away from the house and made their way to the seaside. They got casual work in pubs or on building sites. Lennie was happy. They got by. In two years they lived in six different places.

Sometimes people told George to leave Lennie and go off on his own. "That guy holds you back," they said. But George could never leave him. Since his dad died Lennie was all the family he had.

Now Lennie had finished the kids' game on George's phone. "Tell me about the record shop, George," he said.

"What?"

"The record shop," Lennie said again. "Tell me about it."

George sighed. He must have told Lennie this plan a hundred times.

"OK," he said. "When we get enough money together we're going to rent an empty shop."

"We can get a really good one," Lennie said. "There's loads of empty shops!"

"That's right, and we'll buy records from charity shops and off the internet and sell them on.

We'll have the best second-hand record shop on the south coast."

"And what will we call it, George?"

"We'll call it Lennie's Music Market. And people can come in and sell us records and they can come in and buy records."

"And we'll have coffee," Lennie said.

George nodded. "Free coffee for every customer."

"And doughnuts."

"And doughnuts too, but maybe not free."

"And –"

A knock on the door interrupted them and it opened before George could move to answer it. A young woman stood there. Her wavy hair was up in a ponytail that showed her neck and her dangling earrings in the shape of hearts. She was wearing skinny jeans and a tight yellow jumper. A stack of books was pressed to her chest.

"Hi!" she said, with a wide smile. "I'm Dolly, Boxer's wife. Just wanted to say hello to the new guys."

"Hello!" Lennie said.

He picked up his baseball cap and put it on. Then he took it off again.

"This is a private room," George said.

"Just being friendly," Dolly said.

"What's your books for?" Lennie asked. He stared with wonder at Dolly.

"My homework," she told him. "I'm trying to get in to college, but don't tell you-know-who. Boxer, I mean."

"College ..." Lennie said as he looked Dolly up and down.

"Yeah, I left school too early," Dolly told him. "I got married, see? Now I want to go back and learn. Then I want to be a nursery school teacher. But don't say a word."

She put one finger over her lips just like a teacher in front of a class of little children. Then she turned and left. For a few moments neither George nor Lennie said anything. Then Lennie paced over to the window and started to hum.

A while later the door flew open. This time nobody bothered to knock.

Boxer stood there, with his arms crossed and narrow eyes.

"Was my wife just here?" he said.

"She came and said hello," George said. "She went downstairs, I think."

Boxer stood at the door. Lennie began to fiddle with his shaving things, moving them around on the window sill.

"This room is private," George said for the second time.

"Stay away from my wife," Boxer said.

George opened his mouth to answer, but Boxer was gone.

George shut the door. It needed a lock, but for now he placed his record box in front of it to stop anyone else coming in.

5
THE MANAGER

George was in the back room of the pub, stacking his records in the order he wanted to play them. He held each circle of black vinyl by its rim, so as not to leave finger marks on the shiny surface. When he was finished, he began to sort out the sound equipment.

He had his first set that evening. "Make it good," Billy had told him as he put a sign up outside the pub – *Vintage Sounds Saturday 10 till 12.*

George was whistling to himself when a young man in a smart suit with an open-necked shirt came up to him. George wondered what he was doing in the pub – he looked like he was on his way to a job interview.

"Hi, I'm Danny," the guy said. "I work behind the bar. Some nights I do the door as well."

Danny smiled and held out a bottle of beer for George. George took it, but he felt wary.

"What's up? Not used to seeing a black man in a suit?" Danny posed and smiled as if he was a model.

"No, it's not that!" George couldn't explain. He just wasn't used to such a warm welcome from someone he didn't know.

"Don't worry about it, mate. You're George, the new DJ?" Danny said.

"Yep."

"You going to bring a bit of life back into the pub? It sure as hell needs it."

"Maybe," George said. He gulped back the beer, enjoying the cold fizz as it went down his throat. "Thanks for the beer."

Danny nodded at the racks of vinyl. "What music you playing? Mind if I have a look?"

"Sure."

"These are proper old!" Danny said. "The punters here will like them. I go for more modern stuff myself."

"They're classics!" George protested.

"Sure," Danny said with a grin. "OK if I have your mobile number? I need it for the bar rota."

George reeled off his number and Danny tapped it into his phone.

"Thanks. How about the big lad?"

"He hasn't got a phone," George said. "He's always with me."

Danny smiled his easy grin again. "He's not with you now. He's looking at the dogs."

"Again?" George shook his head, then spoke under his breath, "Lennie! Lennie!"

"It's all right," Danny said. "The dogs are in a cage. They can't hurt him."

"As long as they haven't got puppies, right?" George said.

"All male," Danny said. "Hunting dogs."

'Thank God!' George thought. When he'd first seen the dogs he'd made sure there were no puppies. You couldn't trust Lennie around puppies.

At that point, the doors of the pub opened and Billy and Boxer came in. George felt his body tense and so he squatted down beside the sound system and tried to make sense of the wires and plugs. Danny stood by and watched him. He didn't seem at all worried that the boss had come in and he wasn't doing anything.

Billy was holding a black hold-all with both hands, as though it held something important. Boxer had his phone up to his ear. When he turned to say something to his dad, George noticed that he was wearing cowboy boots with heels. 'Maybe he doesn't like looking small next to his dad,' George thought.

Billy walked towards them, but Boxer stayed where he was, facing the bar and talking on his phone.

"All right, Georgie?" Billy said.

"Good, yeah," said George

"I see you've met my manager, Danny."

"Manager?" George said.

Danny and Billy laughed. Then Billy handed Danny the hold-all and Danny took it with both hands too. Billy said something and Danny nodded and walked off up the stairs with the bag. Boxer was still by the bar shouting into his phone. Billy spotted George looking at him.

"He's booking a holiday," Billy said. "Dolly wants to go to Ibiza to work on her tan. That boy would do anything for her. You got a girlfriend, Georgie?"

"No," George said, and shook his head.

"Lots of nice girls round here."

As Billy walked away, George thought of Lauren again. He remembered her long curly hair which she had hated and tried to straighten all the time. And her gorgeous smile with the gap between the two front teeth. George had liked her a lot, but after his dad died and Lennie started to hang around with him all the time she got fed up. One day he saw her with another lad, someone he didn't know. She had the other lad's jacket round her and her hair was wild with curls. George wondered if the lad had told her that he liked it better curly.

The thought of him whispering that to her gave George a sharp jolt of pain between his ribs.

There hadn't been any other girls since then.

Just him and Lennie.

6
DOGS

A few days later George went out into the yard. He found Lennie sitting with crossed legs by the cages, his face flat up against the wire. A sign above his head said *Beware!*

The dogs in the cages looked like mongrels, with short hair and with big, square jaws. One of them was so skinny that his ribs showed under his coat. He was pacing to and fro and the other one was eating an old trainer. George watched as it grabbed the side of the shoe with its teeth and shook its head from side to side as it tried to tear it apart.

"That one's Paddy and the other is Buzz," Lennie said.

George noticed that Buzz had lost half of one ear. He wondered what kind of hunting these dogs did.

"Have you finished moving the barrels from the cellar?" he asked Lennie.

"All of them," Lennie said, and he pointed at two rows of barrels piled up along the wall.

The back door of the pub opened and Danny came out. Today he was wearing a pale grey suit. The jacket buttons were done up and he looked as neat as if he worked in a bank.

"All right, George? Lennie?" Danny said.

Lennie smiled at Danny.

"He's your cousin?" Danny asked. "Only that's what Billy said."

George nodded but didn't offer any more information. He didn't like talking to people about Lennie. Best to keep family stuff to yourself. Otherwise social workers and all sorts might get involved.

"How come you work for Billy?" George asked.

“I was homeless. Fell out with my family,” Danny said. “Did some bad things, drugs and that. That’s when I met Billy. He got me somewhere to stay and gave me a job. He told me to dress smart. None of your street stuff. If I wear that, the police get on my case, like every other black man round here. So I wear suits and stay off the drugs. Music’s my thing now, and last I heard they can’t arrest you for your taste in music –”

Danny grinned at George then nodded over at Lennie. “How come you were worried about puppies?” he said, his voice low.

“Lennie loves puppies. Trouble is, he’s too strong for them. He might hurt one.”

George remembered the puppies at the place they’d stayed before Brighton. Lennie had kept one of them in his coat pocket and petted it and petted it. Trouble was, he’d forgotten that it needed food and it needed its mum. George had found it in the pocket of Lennie’s coat, a few days later, dead.

“No way he’d hurt these dogs. More like the other way round,” Danny said.

The gate to the yard opened and Dolly came in.

"Hi, guys," she said.

She was wearing a long dress down to her ankles, with a pattern of butterflies. In one hand she was carrying a big pink bag with some books and a furry pencil case sticking out of it. She looked completely out of place in the drab yard.

"What you up to?" she said.

"Just chatting, Doll," Danny said. "Been to the library?"

"Yep! Don't say anything!"

She had her heart-shaped earrings on again and a heart-shaped pendant on a chain round her neck. George wondered if Boxer had bought them for her.

"See you later!" Dolly said and went into the pub. Moments later a window opened upstairs. They all looked up and saw Boxer glaring down at them.

"What you doing?" he demanded.

"Just taking a break," George said. He felt uneasy at the idea that Boxer had been watching out the window, waiting for his wife.

There was a bang as the window slammed shut.

"Boxer's in a bad mood," Danny said. "Again."

George nodded. It seemed like Boxer was always in a bad mood.

7
THE SHOP

They'd been in Hastings for nearly three weeks. For three Saturday nights George had DJ-ed and it had gone well. The drinkers had liked his choice of music and he had played their requests. Even Danny had said, "Not bad, not bad." The rest of the week he'd helped behind the bar. The work wasn't so bad.

Lennie had been busy with the heavy lifting and lugging stuff about. He was also helping to redecorate a couple of the rooms upstairs.

But, best of all, Boxer wasn't there. He and Dolly had gone to Ibiza for a week's holiday. Without Boxer, the pub was an easy place to be.

Billy was out most of the time and Danny looked after the bar. Even the dogs seemed less snappy.

They'd earned a fair bit of money, which George was keeping safe under a floorboard in the room that he and Lennie slept in.

On Tuesday afternoon, there was nothing doing in the pub, and so George and Lennie walked down to the high street and looked at some empty shops. They stopped outside an old café with its windows boarded up.

George used his sleeve to brush the grime from the door. He could just about see inside. There was a long counter and a couple of tables with chairs. There was plenty of space for records, plus they could serve the coffee and doughnuts that Lennie was so keen on.

"Look here, George," Lennie said, and he pointed to a card that was stuck on the door.

SHOP TO LET – Cheap Rent. There was a phone number too. George was about to put it in his mobile when he heard a voice from behind.

"What you doing?"

They turned and saw Danny standing there.

“Just ...” George started.

“We’re going to open a shop,” Lennie butted in. “It’ll be called Lennie’s Music Market. We’re going to sell records and coffee and doughnuts. Aren’t we, George?”

George made a *tsk* sound. He’d told Lennie not to tell anyone.

“Really?” Danny said. He looked at the run-down shop.

“Maybe,” George mumbled. “It depends.”

“Lots of empty shops round here,” Danny said. “Where would you get the stock for it?”

“You know ... off the internet,” George said. “Charity shops. Loads of people want to get rid of vinyl.”

“True,” Danny said with a nod. “Not a bad idea – but you need loads of people to want to buy it too ...”

George knew he was right. “What you up to?” he asked, to change the subject.

“Just off on an errand for Billy,” Danny said. “I’m late so I’d better get going.”

Danny walked off. George watched him go and wondered what Billy had asked him to do. Was it drugs? Billy did seem to have a lot of money. He paid them well and he drove a big white SUV.

He could ask Danny, but then again George sensed that Danny was like two different people. One Danny was the manager of Billy's pub and that seemed to mean looking after the black hold-all and running errands round town. The other Danny was a cool guy in a suit who loved music, always had the time to chat to George and was nice to Lennie.

George wasn't quite sure which one of these was the real Danny.

8
BOXER

On Friday, the day before George's next DJ set, Boxer and Dolly came back from holiday. George was behind the bar when he saw a cab pull up outside the pub and Boxer and Dolly got out. Moments later they were carrying bags along the street and then coming in the side door of the pub.

George looked over at Lennie, who was eating his lunch on a table in the corner of the bar and watching the big-screen TV on the wall. In front of him was a huge bottle of ketchup. He looked really happy, but George had a sick, nervous feeling in his stomach. He stepped out from behind the bar and started to collect empty glasses.

The door from upstairs opened and Dolly burst into the bar, with a clatter from her high-heeled sandals. Her hair was piled up on top of her head, and curly strands hung round her face. Her bare legs and arms were as smooth and golden as honey.

"Hi, everyone! We're back," she called out.

Boxer stood at the door and looked around at the drinkers in the pub. He screwed his nose up as if he smelled something bad.

"Where's Dad?" he said.

"Out on an errand," Danny said. "How was Ibiza?"

"All right, I suppose."

Dolly stood in the middle of the bar, twirling her dress. "What does everyone think of my tan?" she asked.

George noticed that most of the drinkers looked away or down at their phones. But Lennie was still eating. His eyes never left the TV screen as he forked up chips and dipped them into ketchup. He hadn't even noticed Dolly come in.

"Hey, what's wrong with you?"

Boxer was standing in front of George.

"You can't answer my wife when she asks a question?" he said.

"What question?" George said.

"She asked you about her tan," Boxer snarled. "Have you got no manners?"

"Boxer, it wasn't a proper question," Dolly said. She put her hand on Boxer's arm. "I didn't expect an answer. I was just ..."

"Nice tan," George said.

He stepped to one side of Boxer and put the empty glasses on the bar. He took his time and made sure they were all in a straight line. Danny was watching with a wary look on his face. George had his back to Boxer and he could feel the man's eyes drilling into him.

"I don't get you," Boxer said.

George felt the air around him stiffen. Chair legs scraped the floor as if some of the drinkers were moving away.

"You can't be pleasant when me and my wife have been away for a week?" Boxer said. His voice built to a shout. "You can't say something polite?"

George closed his eyes. If he got into a row with Boxer now that would be the end of this job and they would be homeless again. He turned to face Boxer.

"Sorry, mate," he said. "Dolly, your tan is great. You look like you both had a good time."

George's eyes met Boxer's. He tried his hardest to fix the right look on his face. He must have blinked too hard or maybe his eyes shifted a bit. Boxer wasn't fooled.

"Now you're taking the piss!"

George felt his mouth go dry. *Keep calm, keep calm ...*

"Boxer, mate," he began. "Why would I ..."

Boxer placed his phone on the bar. He took a deep breath as if he was very sad about something. Then his arm swung back and before George knew it Boxer's right fist flew round and hit him just below the ear. George felt the punch crunch into his cheekbone and he stumbled to the side. He used his elbows to push Boxer away but he must have caught his leg against a bar stool because he tripped and fell, and his shoulder hit the floor. He braced himself for a kick but nothing came. The next thing he heard was a howling sound like an animal with its leg caught in a trap.

He scrambled to his feet.

Lennie had Boxer by the hand. Boxer's back was up against the bar and glasses were skidding away and smashing onto the floor. Boxer was screaming out to Dolly, to Danny, while he scrabbled with his other hand to try to prise open Lennie's fingers.

George's heart sank. "Lennie, let go!" he yelled.

Boxer's face was frozen with shock, as if a car was about to run him down. Lennie's hand was still clamped tight over his fingers.

"Stop it! Stop it!" Dolly cried

"He'll break his hand!" Danny shouted.

"LENNIE, LET GO OF HIS HAND!" George yelled, louder this time.

But Lennie didn't hear him. He was in a world of his own. His face was blank with hurt and pain. George knew why. Anyone who hurt George hurt Lennie much, much more. He grabbed Lennie's other arm as if he wanted to climb up it and he put his mouth to Lennie ear.

"Please please, Lennie, let go of his hand," he said, in as soft a voice as he could manage.

Lennie let go.

Boxer let out a gurgling sound and cradled his hand as he slid down the bar. His mouth opened as if he was going to cry out, but his voice was gone. Dolly sank down beside him.

"He hit you," Lennie said, and he shook his head as if to clear it.

"Come on," George said. "Let's get out of here."

9

BILLY BELL

George dragged Lennie up the stairs to the bedroom. Lennie was stumbling and silent and George wondered if he understood what he'd done. He walked over to the window and saw the white SUV pull up outside the back gate. It wouldn't be long before Billy Bell found out what had happened.

Then there would be trouble. Real trouble.

"Lennie, we need to go," George said. "Get your bag. Start packing."

There was a knock at the door. It was Danny, banging his knuckles against the palm of his other hand.

"Dolly's taken Boxer to A and E in a taxi," he said. "His hand looks like it's in a bad way."

George shrugged. How could he explain how strong Lennie was? How loyal? The way he was like a child who held on tight and hit out when things went wrong?

"Dolly's furious with Boxer for starting it," Danny said. "Everyone is mad at him."

"Billy's just turned up," George said. "Me and Lennie need to get out of here."

Danny shook his head. "No, don't. I'll tell him what happened. I'll explain. He knows what Boxer's like."

"Yeah, but Boxer's his son," George said. "It won't matter who started it if his son's hurt."

"Billy's not an idiot," Danny said. "Boxer's got a temper, he knows that. He likes you. He likes the pub having a DJ. Let me talk to him, before you start packing."

George nodded and the door closed. He heard Danny's footsteps going downstairs. He sat on the bed and waited.

"Chips," Lennie said. "I didn't finish my chips."

An hour later, Billy Bell asked for George to come and see him in his living room above the main bar. Danny went with him.

Billy was there, sitting on a leather sofa. George noticed the black hold-all tucked away at the side of the sofa.

On the walls were framed photos of Boxer in the boxing ring, with his fists up to his chin in a classic boxer's pose. In another one Boxer was holding a silver cup above his head.

George stood in the middle of the room and looked down at his feet. It was as if he was back in school, standing in front of the Head Teacher. Danny stayed by the door.

"Sit down, Georgie," Billy said.

"I'll stand," George said.

"Boxer's hurt bad," Billy said. His face was hard.

"I know. I don't know what to say," George said. "My cousin doesn't always understand ..."

Billy broke in. "Understanding's got nothing to do with it. You tell me why I shouldn't get my blokes to give your cousin a good kicking."

"He doesn't mean anything bad by it ..."

"He broke Boxer's fingers," Billy said. "How's that going to look? Billy Bell's son got beaten up by a half-wit and he did nothing about it."

"He's not a half-wit!" George burst out.

"You're in no position to get offended, son."

George looked round at Danny. Had he brought George here to get slagged off? So Billy could threaten him?

Danny did a 'sorry' shrug.

"My cousin's not very bright," George said. He tried to keep his voice firm. "But he's loyal to me. He can't cope if he sees me get hurt. Your son hit me first."

George's hand went up to his cheek. Billy nodded.

"And if you set your men on my cousin they'll have to get past me first," George said.

Billy let out a laugh.

"No offence, Georgie, but you're not much of a fighter. Is he, Danny?"

George could hear Danny laughing behind him. The mood in the room got a little bit lighter. Billy sat forward, his elbows on his knees.

"My son's always the first to start a fight," he said. "It's why I got him into the boxing when he was a lad. But that all finished a few years ago and now he's just quick to flare up, too fast with his fists. I know. Danny's told me. Other people as well. People I trust."

"I'm sorry ..." George began.

Billy waved his hand.

"Your cousin's fast with his fists, too," he said. "Maybe I could use him. Sometimes, if a deal doesn't go right, I need someone to sort things out for me."

George knew what Billy meant. He wanted Lennie to put the boot in for him. He shook his head.

"I could make it worth his while," Billy said. "I'm not short of a few bob."

"Lennie's soft," George said. "He's not an animal. The only time he gets upset is if someone has a go at me. He wouldn't hit anyone else."

Billy pursed his lips. George had that back-at-school feeling again.

"If you want we can leave," George said.

"I like that you're loyal," Billy said. "I like that your cousin's loyal. I'd like to think you might both be loyal to me. And you're good workers. Can you keep him out of trouble?"

"I can."

"You can both stay on for a while," Billy said. "Boxer and Dolly are moving anyway. He's looking after a club I run in Bexhill and so he won't be around. If you do see him just steer clear."

"I will," George promised. "We will. I'll make sure Lennie stays out of trouble."

"You do that."

George left the room. As he walked along the hall he felt his heart thump in his chest. He put his hand over it. He needed to calm down. Everything was all right. He would forget that Billy had called Lennie a half-wit. He had to let that go because, after all, Lennie had broken his son's fingers. They would stay in the pub for the next few weeks and then they would rent a shop. Then they'd be their own bosses and life would be a lot easier.

10

DOLLY

A few days later, George was going upstairs to his room when he heard a woman's voice singing, clear and light. He walked along the landing and saw that the door to Boxer and Dolly's bedroom was open. He knew that Boxer wasn't around – he'd seen him leave in a van earlier.

He looked into the room and saw Dolly there, standing by a table piled high with books and papers. It was the first time he'd seen her since Lennie broke her husband's fingers. She was wearing cut-off shorts and a striped T-shirt. The heart-shaped pendant sat at her neck.

She looked round at him. "Just packing a few books for Bexhill," she said.

She put a ring binder in her pink bag, then wedged the furry pencil case in beside it. Her wavy hair was tucked behind her ears. She didn't have any make-up on, which made her look like a young girl, not a married woman.

"How do you put up with Boxer?" George asked. All of a sudden he needed to know.

"He's not all bad," she said.

George touched his cheek. It still hurt.

"I saw what he did – and he deserved what he got," she said. "I don't blame Lennie. But sometimes Boxer comes across wrong. He can be sweet."

George rolled his eyes.

"He can!" she said.

"Sweet or not, why did you hook up with him?" he asked. "You're just a kid. How old is he? Thirty?"

"I'm 19. Not so young."

'Young enough,' George thought. She was the same age as him.

"Boxer rescued me," Dolly said.

"Rescued you?" George said.

"About a year ago I had this big fight with my stepdad and he threw me out. It was midnight and I had nowhere to go. I ended up sitting on the seafront at Eastbourne. It was freezing cold and this car pulled up and there was Boxer. He took his coat off and put it round me. He brought me here and I stayed in your room upstairs for weeks. Then he asked me to marry him."

George didn't know what to say. Billy Bell had rescued Danny. Now Boxer had done the same for Dolly.

"I suppose you think I shouldn't have married him," Dolly said. "But he looked after me. He still does, most of the time."

"What about college?" George asked.

"He doesn't want me to go," she said. She looked down at her feet. "He says I don't need to work. But I'm going to be a brilliant teacher. He'll be proud of me."

George pictured Boxer in his cowboy boots standing next to his father. His father was taller, more powerful. Maybe Boxer needed this young wife so he could boss her about, be more powerful than someone else.

"I know you don't like him," Dolly said. "Not many people do. But he loves me and I'll get to college in the end."

"What about your mum?" George asked. "What does she think?"

Dolly looked angry. "My mum doesn't think about me at all. She's too busy thinking about my stepdad. He hated me. Life's better here than it was at my mum's house."

"But you're just a kid," George said. "Wouldn't you rather be free?"

"Free?" she snapped. "Like you're free? Looking after your cousin 24/7 ..."

Dolly snatched up her bag and George stepped back to let her pass. He could hear her heels clicking all the way down the stairs.

11

THE BLACK HOLD-ALL

That Saturday night, Lennie was in the bedroom watching TV and George was DJ-ing.

He was all sorted with his records lined up in his box and his headphones on. As one track played he'd put a second one on the other turntable. And then as soon as the first track finished the other one would start, edging its way into the beat of the original. It was all going great and he was pleased that a few people were dancing, shuffling and jigging in time to the music.

And then a fight broke out between two young men. Before George had time to think, other people joined in and the room was full of shouting and screaming.

Tables and chairs toppled over and some people ended up on the floor. Then Billy Bell appeared.

He strode into the middle of the fighters. Danny and a couple of the other barmen followed him. George turned the music off and jumped out from behind the decks to help. Danny grabbed his arm and shouted in his ear.

"Go behind the bar. *Now.* In case someone tries to rob us."

George rushed over to the bar and turned the pub lights on. Everywhere was lit up with a harsh yellow light. People blinked and put their hands over their eyes. The light showed just how shabby the pub was and made everyone look ten years older. Billy was marching one man out of the door – the man's arm was twisted up behind his back. Danny walked past with another one. People drifted back to their tables and there were calls of *Turn the lights down!* and *What happened to the music?*

"Shall I call the police?" George said.

Danny shook his head. "Billy'll deal with it."

George dimmed the lights again and a couple of the bar staff joined him and began serving drinks. George was about to go back to the decks when he saw the black hold-all down the side of the bar.

George picked it up and took it back to his DJ stage. He put it by the speakers for safe keeping and turned the decks on. From time to time he looked over at the exit to see if Billy or Danny were coming back in. There was no sign of them. Soon the pub got back to normal. George turned the music up loud and people started dancing again.

George squatted down behind the turntables and unzipped the black hold-all.

He'd expected to see plastic bags, hundreds of them, each holding a few pills or a spoonful of white powder. Instead he saw a towel. Confused, he felt around it. Something hard was wrapped up inside it. He stood up for a moment and set the next record to play. Over by the door he saw Billy coming in, followed by Danny. Billy was laughing at something.

George had to know what was in the bag.

He bent down again as if he was sorting out the wires. He put his hand into the bag and moved the edges of the towel. He looked up to make sure Billy and Danny were over the other side of the pub. Then he looked down again.

What he saw sent a prickle of fear down his spine. He knew Billy was involved in some shady stuff, but this was something else.

A gun. Black, smooth and heavy.

He tucked the towel back round it and zipped the hold-all up. He stood up and put another record on, not paying any attention to how well it gelled with the one before.

After a few more tracks, Danny walked across to him.

"You looking for that?" George said, and he nodded at the hold-all on the floor. "I saw it over by the bar and I thought I'd better keep it safe."

"Thanks, mate," Danny said, and wiped pretend sweat off his forehead.

He took the hold-all and walked away.

As George watched him go, he wondered if he knew what he was carrying.

12

THE GUN

Lennie was asleep when George went upstairs. He sat on the side of his bed and untied his boots.

He thought of the black hold-all and what had been inside.

It wasn't the first gun George had seen.

That was when he was 15 and hung around with a kid called Tommy Black. Tommy had an older brother, Brett, who'd been in and out of prison. Tommy was always telling stories about what his brother got up to in prison, the fights and the scams and the drugs.

One day, in the summer holidays, Tommy texted George and asked him to meet up by the old factories. When George turned up, Tommy had his school rucksack over his shoulder. George wanted to laugh. He was going to say, *What's this? Homework club?* when Tommy pulled him over to the doors of the derelict factory. He put his hand into the rucksack and pulled out a gun. It was small and silver and looked just like the ones that George had seen in films and on TV. "It's not loaded," Tommy had told him. "But it's real!"

Tommy said his brother had showed him how to shoot and so he taught George how to hold the gun, how to check whether there were bullets in it. He showed him how to pull the trigger.

They'd walked round with it all afternoon, taking turns to hold it in their pockets. George had pointed the gun at the old factories, at the doors and windows, then pulled the trigger – *Pow!* They chased each other around the waste ground. After a few hours Tommy put the gun back into his rucksack.

After that, whenever George saw Tommy from across the playground, Tommy would smile and make his hand into the shape of a gun, then he'd point the two fingers at George and mouth the word *Pow!*

The gun in the black hold-all looked different to Brett's gun, but George was sure it was real. He wondered about the men that Billy and Danny had hauled out of the pub earlier. Billy and Danny had been gone for ages and then they'd come back in laughing like two blokes sharing a big secret.

Just how violent were they? Billy seemed like the sort of person who would use a gun if pushed. But Danny? Would he go along with random violence like that?

13
GOING OUT

Despite the fight, the pub felt calmer and safer after Boxer and Dolly had gone. For the next few days Lennie was either decorating the upstairs rooms or sitting in the back yard talking to the dogs. George was doing extra shifts behind the bar.

The money was stacking up and George was putting it all under the floorboard in his bedroom. It was more than they'd ever saved before.

On that Friday Danny asked George to go for a drink with him at a pub by the pier.

George finished his shift, had a shower and got changed. He kept looking out the window down at Lennie who was sorting out the barrels in the back yard and talking to the dogs. The bar staff had said they would keep an eye on him for an hour or so. As George got dressed he realised that this was the first time he'd gone out on his own for years.

He stood in front of the mirror. He looked neat. Lauren used to say that he was good looking – and sometimes that made her jealous of other girls, in case he might go off with one of them. But George wasn't interested in anyone else. He liked Lauren even though she had a gap in her front teeth. No, he liked her because she had a gap in her front teeth.

It was almost five. George put some money in his wallet and went downstairs to the pub. Danny was waiting by the door. This time he looked like a salesman in a dark suit with a white T-shirt underneath.

They sat at a table outside the pub with a pint of beer each and talked about music. When they fell quiet, George looked out to sea.

"What do you know about Billy Bell?" Danny asked, in a low voice.

George thought about the gun in the black hold-all. "I know he does illegal stuff. Drugs, I think. And I bet he's no stranger to violence."

"Violence, yes," Danny said. "But he doesn't do drugs. At least, he doesn't sell them."

"So where does he make his money?" George asked. "It can't be from the pub."

"No." Danny looked about, as if he wanted to check no one was listening. "Look," he said. "There's stuff I'm going to tell you. I want to put a proposal to you."

George shook his head. "I can't do anything dodgy," he said. "I've got Lennie to look after. If I got nicked he just wouldn't cope. I can't ..."

"No, I don't mean I want you to do anything with Billy," Danny said. "It's something different. Billy's been good to me. He pays me well. He doesn't expect me to do any hands-on stuff ... But the truth is I've had enough of working for the guy."

George drank his beer and waited to see what Danny had to say.

"He's involved with some big-time criminals," he went on. "He does their dirty work for them. Sorts out people they want to punish."

George thought of the gun again.

"He kills people?" he asked.

"No, he punishes them," Danny said. "The people he works for, they're drug dealers in London. When someone causes them trouble they drive them down to Hastings and Billy deals with them."

"He gives them a good kicking," George said. He remembered what Billy had threatened to do to Lennie.

"Sometimes," Danny said. "Sometimes he might use weapons, hurt someone bad. But most times he just frightens them."

Danny paused and drank some beer. "I need to get away from him," he said. "I can't take it any more. The other week, late at night, he took me out. Put the dogs in the back of the car and drove to the cliffs. I thought I'd done something to upset him. But then this car pulls up and a kid gets out. No more than 16. He was terrified. Sweating and shaking and blubbing for his mum."

George pushed his beer away. He didn't like what he was hearing. He just wanted to work at the pub for four more weeks. He didn't want anything to get in the way of that.

But Danny went on with his story.

"This kid had been ripping off a London dealer," he said. "The people in the car drove away. The lad was standing there, shaking. I thought I was going to have to watch him get a kicking. But it was worse than that."

"Billy said to the kid, *Start running. I'll count to ten then I let the dogs go*. The lad got down on his knees and begged him not to do it, but he just started counting. When he got to eight the kid got up and started to run."

Danny flexed his shoulders and undid his suit jacket as if it was too tight for him all of a sudden.

"He let the dogs go."

George gasped. He pictured the dogs tearing across the grass.

"Did they catch him?" he asked.

"I didn't wait to find out," Danny said. "I walked off. I hitched a lift and got back here before Billy. When he came back he was all laughing. He said it was only a game but ..."

"You don't know what happened to the kid?"

Danny shook his head.

"I didn't ask. But I've had enough. I'm going to leave the pub and Hastings. That's what I wanted to talk to you about. I like your idea about renting a shop, making a business. A legit business."

George was still thinking about the boy on the cliffs, the dogs tearing after him. The horror of it gave him a sick feeling in his stomach.

"I've got almost £5,000 saved," Danny said. "A proper whack of money. I could start a business myself but it'd be more fun to do it with you guys. I could come in with you. The three of us could open a shop, buy the stock. Like Lennie said."

"I don't know ..." George began.

The record shop had just been for him and Lennie. He'd never thought about someone else being involved. In any case, what Danny had just told him about Billy had made him look at Danny in a different light. He might not like it, but Danny was part of Billy's world. Now he wanted to be part of George and Lennie's world.

"I'd have to think about it," he said.

"Course," Danny said. "No rush."

George swigged the rest of his beer. "I should get back."

Danny pushed his glass away and did his jacket up again.

"It could be good. A new start. The three of us running the shop. Course we'd need some modern music as well as your stuff," he said with a smile.

14

LENNIE

The Old Ship Inn was quiet.

Danny went behind the bar, but George headed upstairs. When he got to the landing he saw Dolly's pink bag by the banister. She must have come back from Bexhill to get something. George hoped Boxer wasn't with her. He walked up the next flight of stairs in a gloomy mood.

The talk with Danny had depressed him. The things he'd told him about Billy Bell were grim. Then there was his offer to put his £5,000 into Lennie's Music Market. It was all too much. George's head felt heavy and fogged up with stuff that shouldn't be there.

He found Lennie lying on the bed, with his face pressed into the pillow. He was awake, but hiding. He only did that when he was upset about something. George felt a stab of guilt. He'd gone out with Danny and left him. Had Lennie thought he wasn't coming back? Had he just got sad like he sometimes did?

George sat on his own bed and reached across and touched Lennie's arm. "What's up?"

When Lennie didn't respond, he took hold of his arm and pulled so that his hand came away from his face.

Lennie was crying.

"What's the matter?" George said. "What's happened?"

Lennie shook his head and tried to turn away.

"Has someone said something? Was Boxer here?"

Lennie put his hand in front of his face again.

Then George saw the chain with the heart dangling on it. It was lying on the pillow near

Lennie's hand and George could see that the chain was around his little finger.

"Where did you get this?" George asked. He unwound the chain and lifted it away from Lennie. "Did you take this from Dolly? Did you steal it?"

George stood up.

"Lennie, get up. We have to give this back." He didn't know what had happened but he knew that it was important to put it right.

"Why did you do this?" he asked. "Lennie, why? You've never stolen anything before."

Lennie got up off the bed. He was still crying, his body letting out little shudders. It was a hard thing for George to watch.

"Come on," he said. "Dolly's nice. She'll be OK about it."

He walked downstairs with heavy steps. He saw that Dolly's bag was still on the landing, so she hadn't left yet. He went towards her old room. Lennie lagged behind him.

George knocked on the door. No answer. He knocked again. He looked back and saw Lennie standing at the foot of the attic stairs.

"Dolly?" he called out. "Dolly, it's George. I found your chain."

He decided he would say he'd seen it on the landing, and not involve Lennie at all.

"Dolly?" he called.

As he called, Lennie made a sound. A whimper. George looked back at him. There was a bleak look on his face, one that he'd seen before. A look that had been there on the day he'd found the dead puppy in Lennie's coat pocket. George had taken the puppy out. It hadn't been much bigger than his hand and its fur was hard and stiff. Its body was cold and its pink tongue was poking out the side of its mouth.

Lennie had cried and cried.

George looked again at Lennie's face and felt his stomach drop. He pushed the door open but didn't go inside. He just looked into the room from where he was.

Dolly was lying on the floor on her back.

"No," he whispered.

He could hear Lennie crying again, with harsh juddering sobs. He crept into the room. Dolly's hair was loose and her eyes were closed. He touched the warm, soft flesh of her arm. Maybe she was just knocked out. Maybe she'd fallen and hit her head. He put his fingers on her neck to feel her pulse and let them stay there for ten, twenty seconds. His eyes were closed too as he concentrated, trying to feel Dolly's blood pumping round her body.

But there was nothing. No movement, no heartbeat, no breath.

Dolly was dead.

George stood up and stepped back. Lennie was still standing behind him.

"I looked at the chain," Lennie said. "She shouted. I said *Shush* ..."

George couldn't speak. He felt like he was trapped on a wave – the floor was pulsing up and down beneath his feet. He didn't know what to say, what to do. He put his arm out and leaned against the wall. He tried to stand up, to turn away from the body, away from Dolly's soft flesh, her wavy hair and her heart-shaped earrings.

"Lennie ..."

He had to say something, but the words stuck in his throat.

Danny was standing behind Lennie. His face was frozen, his eyes fixed on Dolly's lifeless body.

15

RUNNING AWAY

Danny came into the room and closed the door behind him. He sank down by Dolly's body and touched her face. Then he picked up her arm and felt her wrist. George wanted to tell him that he'd already done it, but the words still wouldn't come. His tongue felt like it was glued to the top of his mouth.

Danny stood up.

"He do this?" he said, pointing at Lennie.

George nodded. Lennie folded his arms.

"You better get him out of here. We need to get out of this room. Let someone else find her ..."

George pushed Lennie out of the door. Danny followed, swearing over and over. Dolly's bag was still on the landing, so Danny picked it up and took it back into the room.

"You need to do something about Lennie," Danny said. "Before Billy or Boxer find her ... They'll know who it was. They'll ask me and I won't be able to lie to them."

George took Lennie's arm and shoved him towards the stairs.

"Downstairs, Lennie, into the yard."

The yard was empty. The cage door was hanging open and the dogs were gone. He took Lennie to the back gate and checked the SUV wasn't there. Out on the street he held onto Lennie's arm as he told him what to do.

"You remember when we were coming here and we stopped that day?" he said. "Remember the hot dog van? Remember we sat on the bench and ate the hot dogs?"

"With ketchup?"

"Yes, with ketchup. Remember the tree? The one with the heart carved into it?"

Lennie nodded.

"Go there now and wait for me," George said. "I might not get there till it's very dark. I'll bring our stuff. We've got to move on."

"Because of Dolly ..."

George nodded. "Don't talk to anyone," he said. His voice was firm and flat. "Just go to that place, near the hot dog van, near the tree with the heart. Sit on that bench. Wait for me. The hot dog van might close and everyone might go home, but you stay there and wait for me."

"OK. I'll wait."

George watched Lennie walk off then he raced up to the attic and started to pack. He needed to get out before Billy came back.

He packed what he could into two rucksacks. He pulled the floorboard up, got the money out and put it in his pocket. Then he heard footsteps coming up to the room. He turned round as Danny pushed the door open.

"I just got a call from Billy," Danny said. "He'll be back in twenty minutes. You need to get away."

"I'm ready," George said.

He looked at his record case. It would have to stay behind. His dad's records were in there, but he couldn't carry them any more.

"You'll have to disappear," Danny said. "I mean it. Billy won't rest till he finds Lennie. He'll scour the country for him."

"What if I took Lennie to the police?" George said. "What if he confessed? They'd protect him. They could see that he's got a disability."

"Billy's got friends," Danny warned him. "Prison or hospital won't help Lennie. Billy'd find him. I've told you what he's like."

"I get it. I'll go."

"Billy will want me with him," Danny said. "But I'll text you. Let you know where he is so you can keep out of his way."

"Thanks."

"I guess there'll be no Lennie's Music Market now."

George shook his head and walked out with his bags. He went down one flight of stairs and stopped. There was something else he needed to take with him. He walked along the hall and into Billy's living room. There it was, by the sofa. The black hold-all. He unzipped it and pulled out the gun in the towel. When he got back out to the hall Danny shook his head.

"That's not a good idea," he said.

"At least he can't shoot Lennie with this," George said.

"There are other guns," Danny said.

"Then I'll need a gun to defend me and Lennie with."

George slipped out of the back door, put his hood up and walked away.

16

LAST DAY IN HASTINGS

George didn't go straight to the meeting place. He ended up walking around in circles, down to the pier then along the front. He went to the high street and stood outside the boarded up café and he thought about Lennie's Music Market.

Now it would never happen. They would have to run from town to town. Billy Bell would never give up looking for Lennie. Even if they could avoid the police, George would always be looking behind him.

At last, he headed out of town to the Snack Attack burger van and the tree with the heart carved in it. But along the way he changed his mind, slowed and walked a different way until he found a little clump of trees. It was gone ten and the night was dark. There was no one around and so George sat with his back to a tree and got the gun out of his rucksack. He kept the towel around it while he checked to see if it was loaded.

It was.

Why had he taken it? Danny said that Billy had other guns. Was George expecting to defend Lennie with it? Was it to be like an old Western where George would draw the gun to give Lennie time to gallop off into the night?

Just then his phone beeped. A message from Danny.

They've found Dolly.

He'd been gone from the pub for over two hours. Billy had had no reason to go into Boxer and Dolly's old room – why would he? Maybe Boxer had turned up at the pub looking for her. When he couldn't find her he'd gone up to the room, opened the door and seen her dead on the floor.

The world tilted. George crossed his arms and leaned forward. His stomach churned. Dolly had planned to go to college and become a teacher.

Dolly with her wavy hair and her heart pendant and earrings. He tried to imagine what might have happened. She'd probably been chatting to Lennie in her nice kind way and the pendant had caught his eye. He'd liked it, had picked it up and looked at it. At first she might not have minded. She might have said, *Oh, this old thing!* But Lennie would have held it for far too long and she'd have tried to uncurl his fingers, move herself away from him.

Lennie would have held on and if she'd screamed Lennie would have put his hand over her mouth.

Take care of Lennie, his dad had said. *Promise me you will.*

But what would his dad have done in a fix like this?

What was George going to do when he met up with Lennie? What was his plan? To jump on a bus and head out of Hastings? He had a few hundred quid, but where would that take them? Would they go to another town and hope Billy wouldn't find them? Or the police? George would live his whole life waiting for Billy Bell to jump out of a car and take his revenge.

What would Billy do? Bundle Lennie into the back of the car, take him up to the top of the cliffs and tell him he was going to count to ten before they set the dogs on him?

How could he let that happen to Lennie? George closed his eyes. He saw a moving picture of Lennie running fast at first then slowing down. Then the dogs, Paddy and Buzz, racing up to him, their teeth like the edges of a saw, their jaws like clamps.

He felt himself shake with fear and cold.

Another text from Danny.

Billy's gone mental. He's got people looking for Lennie.

The words jolted him out of his panic. He had to get a grip. It wouldn't be long until one of Billy's mates saw Lennie sitting on the bench next to Snack Attack. He stood up and started to head back towards the coast. It didn't take long for him to reach the road and further up he could see the outline of the old van where they'd bought the hot dogs. The lights were off – the café was closed for the night.

Lennie was on the bench. George saw his broad back, his square shoulders.

His phone beeped.

Lennie's been seen, on a bench by the shore, on the Brighton road.

George felt his chest tighten. Billy's men were on their way. It wouldn't be long until they were here. He felt in his rucksack for the gun, put it in his pocket and walked towards the bench.

Lennie turned round. His face broke into a smile.

"I waited, George."

George let the rucksacks drop down by the bench.

"I had three hot dogs," Lennie told him. "With ketchup."

Another text.

Coming. Only minutes away.

Soon the SUV would arrive and Billy and Boxer would get out and they would take Lennie from him. George wouldn't be able to save him.

"What shall we do now?" Lennie said.

"We'll just sit here for a minute."

"I've been sitting here for ages, George."

"I know. Just a bit longer."

George felt the gun in his pocket. He thought he could hear dogs barking. But he knew he couldn't – the dogs would be in the back of Billy's car. They wouldn't bark until Billy let them out.

He found himself rocking backwards and forwards. Lennie was talking – his voice was low, a bit odd, as if he was nervous, as if he knew something bad was going to happen. George felt angry with himself. He shouldn't be letting Lennie get upset.

He looked back up the road and saw the white SUV pull up.

A hand seemed to grab at his heart and squeeze it.

George would take care of Lennie. He would make sure that Billy Bell never got hold of him. That's why he had the gun. He would make sure that no one would upset or hurt Lennie ever again.

"Tell me about the record shop," George said.

Lennie turned to him and smiled.

"Well, when we get enough money ..."

"Look over there while you tell me," George said. "Look at the heart on the tree."

Lennie did as he was told and turned away.

"We're going to save up lots of money and then we're going to look for an empty shop. There are lots of empty shops, aren't there, George?"

"There are lots of empty shops ..."

"And you'll buy a load of records off the internet and from charity shops ..."

George glanced round. Billy Bell and Boxer had got out of the SUV and were twenty metres or so away. They started to walk towards him. He turned back to Lennie.

"What about the doughnuts, Lennie?"

"We going to have doughnuts and coffee and ..."

George raised the gun so that it pointed at the back of Lennie's head.

"And we're going to call it Lennie's Music Market ..."

"And what will we do there?"

"We'll sell records and ..."

George pulled the trigger.

He felt himself jerk backwards. Lennie fell forward. His big body slumped over until he was on the ground. George pressed his fist over his mouth.

"What the f ...?"

He heard Boxer's voice. He stood up and swung round with the gun still in his hand. He pointed it at Boxer and Billy and they began to back away. Behind them was Danny.

"George, mate ..."

Danny walked around Billy and Boxer.

"Let it go now," he said to George.

He stepped forward and took the gun from George's hand.

"You've got to get out of here. The police will be here soon. You've got to go."

George looked at Lennie. He'd fallen at an odd angle and was lying humped over, broken and lifeless. The sight of him made George's legs give way. Danny caught him, stopped him from falling.

"Get your stuff and get out of here," Danny whispered.

"Wait a minute ..." Boxer called. "George was involved as well. He can't get away scot free."

"Leave him," Billy said. "It was the cousin."

George picked up the bags.

He put his hood up and headed for the road to Brighton. He left his cousin's body lying on the dark, hard ground.